It's Me, Teddy!

Story by Amber Alexander
Illustrations by Todd Cummings

A Storey Publishing Book

STOREY

Storey Communications, Inc.
Schoolhouse Road
Pownal, Vermont 05261

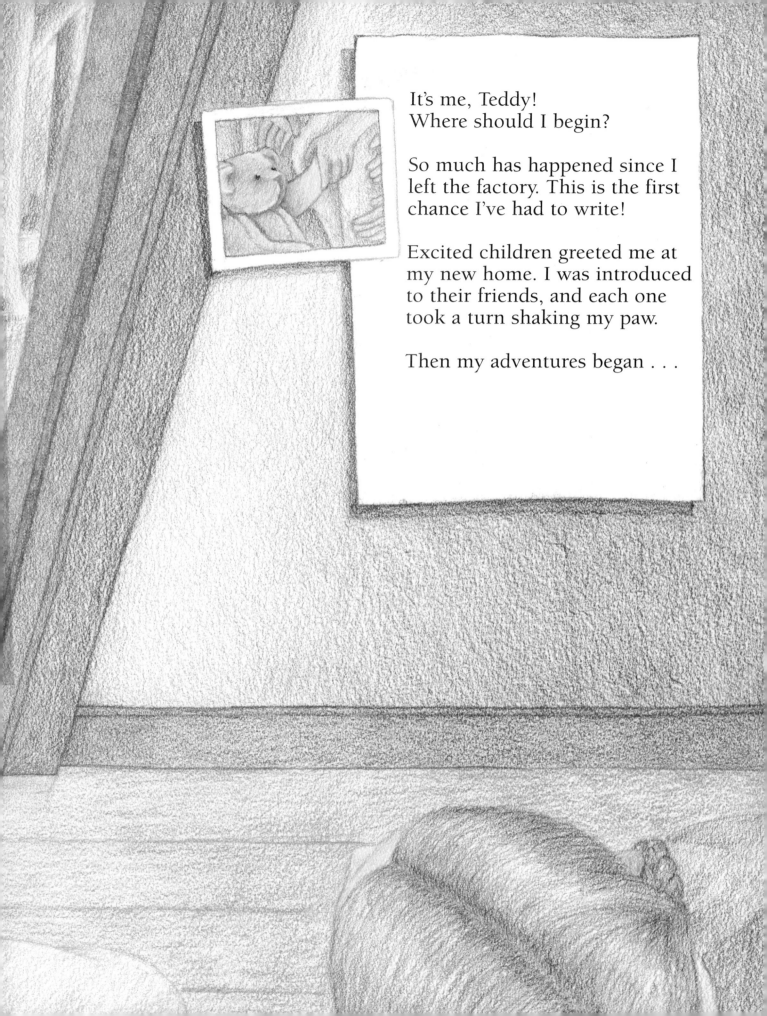

It's me, Teddy!
Where should I begin?

So much has happened since I left the factory. This is the first chance I've had to write!

Excited children greeted me at my new home. I was introduced to their friends, and each one took a turn shaking my paw.

Then my adventures began . . .

First we played beauty parlor.
They powdered me and
painted me, and took turns
doing my fur.

They didn't even charge me
because I told them I left my
wallet back at the factory.

Then they dunked me in a
tub full of warm bubble bath.

All the makeup they had
just put on me was gone in
minutes, and *I* was five
pounds heavier!

That's right—I soaked up
water like a sponge. The
children had to wring
me out!

Once I was dry, the children were ready to play cowboys.

I was the cow.

"Rope that little dowgie before he gets away!" they yelled.

They lassoed me, tied me up, and hung me from a tree. Those children really know how to tie a knot!

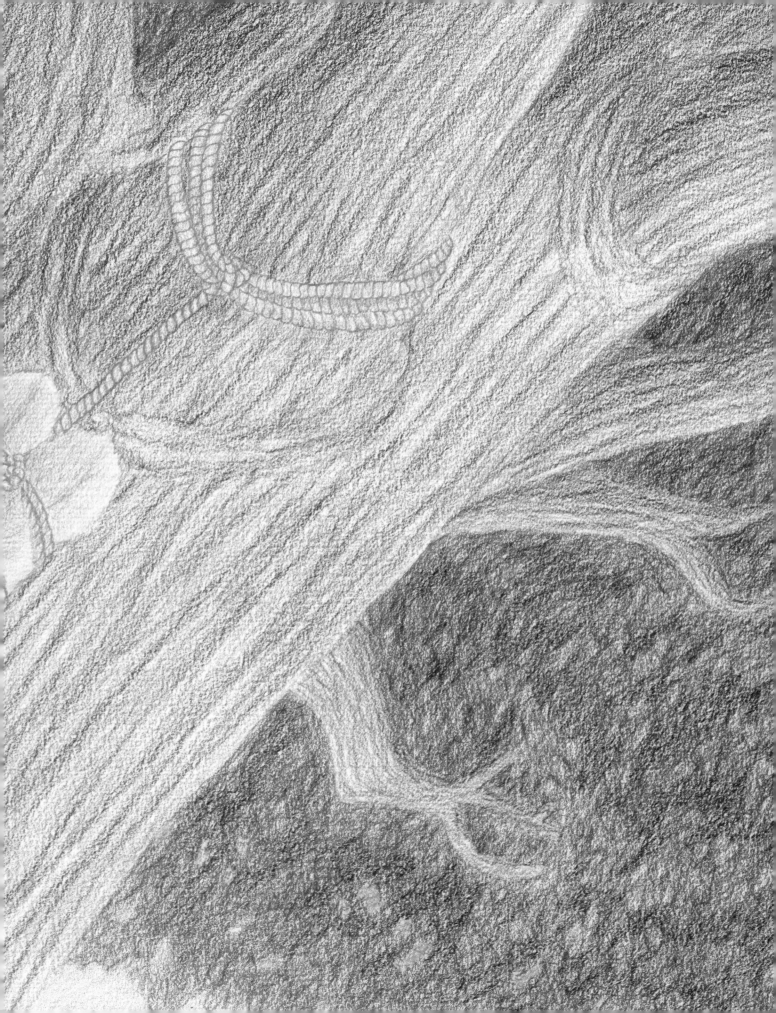

A little later I was able to rest when we played doctor. The children wrapped me in bandages—from head to toe!

"You've had a long day," they said. "You need to rest."

But my day wasn't over yet . . .

"We made you a harness so you can pull our wagon!" shouted the children. And they had—with snaps and buckles in all the right places.

Obviously, they had been planning for my arrival for a long time.

Now, I'm not really a *work bear,* so I just stood there. When they realized we weren't going anywhere, they untied me and tried to hook up the house cat.

It was time for her to wake up, anyway!

Later, it got dark. I thought it might be time to sleep, but there was more . . .

A campfire!

We sat in a circle around the roaring fire. The children roasted marshmallows, and tried to feed them to me by rubbing them all over my face.

I couldn't taste it because I don't have a mouth, but it SMELLED awfully good.

After that, the children went inside to brush their teeth. They wanted to clean mine, too.

"Open up that furry little mouth of yours!" they said. They still didn't seem to understand—I don't HAVE a furry little mouth, or furry little teeth for that matter!

It was bedtime . . .

"We're afraid to close our eyes because of the monster who comes around after dark," one child said.

Don't get me wrong—I was tired, but not too tired to do my bear duty and stand guard ALL NIGHT. The monster didn't dare show his face that night!

Morning came and I was a little tired, but it was a good kind of tired, because I had scared him away!

"Come on, let's go to school, Teddy!" cried the children.

SCHOOL?

I didn't want to be left home alone, so I went. But, secretly, I didn't plan on doing any work.

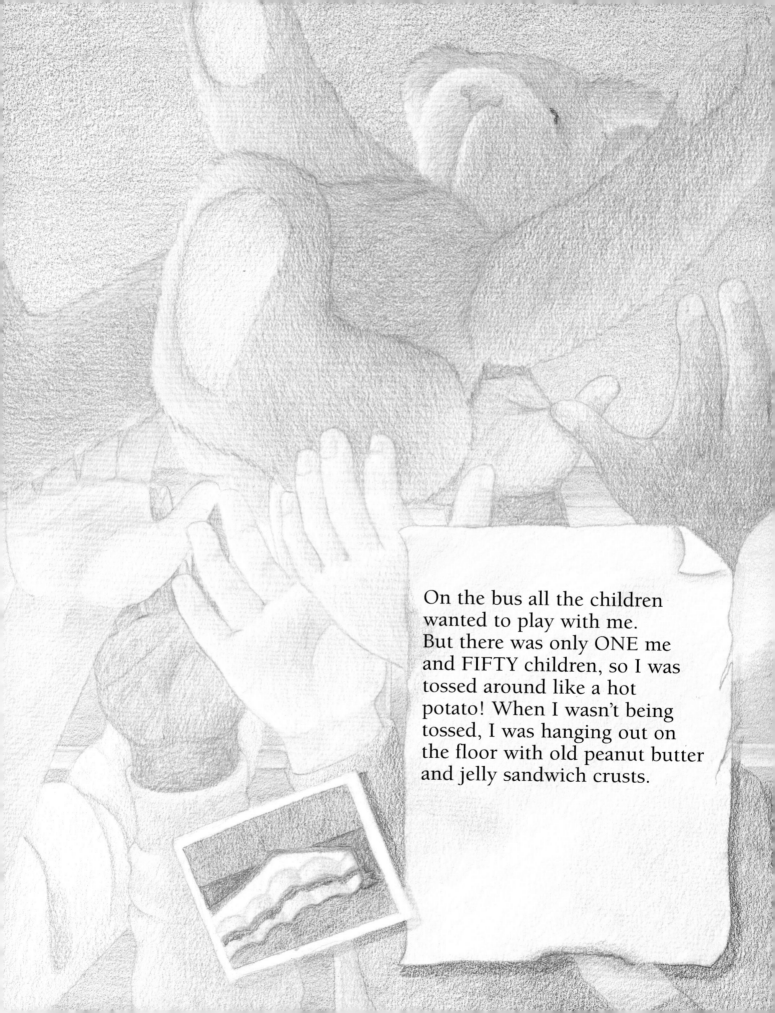

On the bus all the children wanted to play with me. But there was only ONE me and FIFTY children, so I was tossed around like a hot potato! When I wasn't being tossed, I was hanging out on the floor with old peanut butter and jelly sandwich crusts.

In school, the teacher took me from the children and put me in a drawer. She was worried the children wouldn't pay any attention to her with me around.

I got a lot done in the drawer. I made friends with a bullfrog named Joe, learned how to use a slingshot, and caught up on the sleep I missed out on the night before!

After school, the children were ready to play again. One of them produced measuring tape and took my measurements.

I thought, "That's nice, they're making me a dress." But it was better. The next thing I knew, I was fastened to a kite.

"Have you ever tried hang gliding?" they asked, as they gave me a big push out of a second-story window.

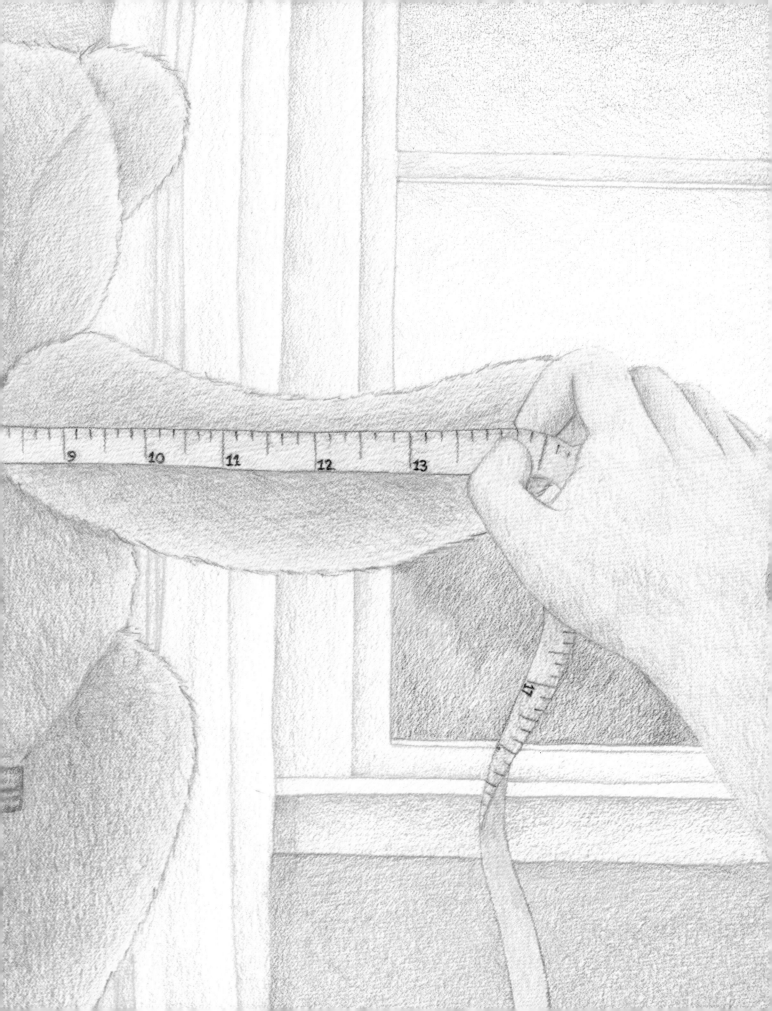

It just so happens, I've always
wanted to know what it would
feel like to fly, and for a second,
I knew . . .

YEE-HAW!

I never believed it when people talked about how bears bounce, but it's true . . .

I bounced! All that stuffing finally paid off!

I landed, and looked up
and saw . . .

enough drool to swim in,
and some very sharp teeth.
And they DID NOT belong to
the children!

Soon I was covered in drool
as a huge, hairy dog carried
me away.

I was scared, but I tried to sit
back and enjoy the ride.

After that, things got a little
blurry. I think I got drool in
my eyes.

But he must have dropped me,
because I'm still in one piece.
Just a little wet!

It's time for bed again, so I have to go. The children are convinced I've gotten rid of the monster for good, so I get to sleep with them tonight.

I overheard one of them talking about tomorrow and by the sound of things, I had better get some sleep.

Being a best friend to this many children is hard work. I LOVE it, but it sure looks like a five bear job to me . . .

COULD YOU PLEASE SEND MORE BEARS?

Your friend,

teddy

P.S. Some clothes would be nice, too. Even the DOG has a sweater.

This book is dedicated to all the teddy bears who have written to us at the factory— and to their owners, who helped them hold the pens.

From: teddy

to:
the Vermont Teddy Bear Co.
2236 Shelburne Rd.
Shelburne, Vermont 05482

The mission of Storey Communications is to serve our customers by publishing practical information that encourages personal independence in harmony with the environment.

Copyright © 1995 by
The Vermont Teddy Bear Company™

It's Me, Teddy! was created and produced in cooperation with The Vermont Teddy Bear Company™ by Storey Communications, Inc., Pownal, Vermont 05261.

Edited by Deborah L. Balmuth
Cover and text design by
  Laurie Musick Wright

Printed in the United States by Excelsior Printing Company
Bound by Horowitz/Rae Book Manufacturers, Inc.
First Printing, July 1995

Library of Congress Cataloging-in-Publication Data

Alexander, Amber, 1968–
    It's me, Teddy! / story by Amber Alexander : illustrations by Todd Cummings.
        p.   cm.
    "A Storey Publishing book."
    Summary: Teddy writes a letter to the other bears at the factory telling of his unpredictable, humorous experiences in his new home.
    ISBN 0-88266-805-6
    [1. Teddy bears—Fiction.   2. Letters—Fiction.]
I. Cummings, Todd, 1967– ill. II. Title.
PZ7.A3763It   1995
[E]—dc20   95-10221
                                            CIP
                                            AC